HEART OF AN OUTCAST MISTRESS

Heart of an Outcast Mistress

A Thaumorian Legends Novella

A M Eno

ISBN
979-8-9893390-8-2 (paperback)
979-8-9893390-9-9 (ebook)

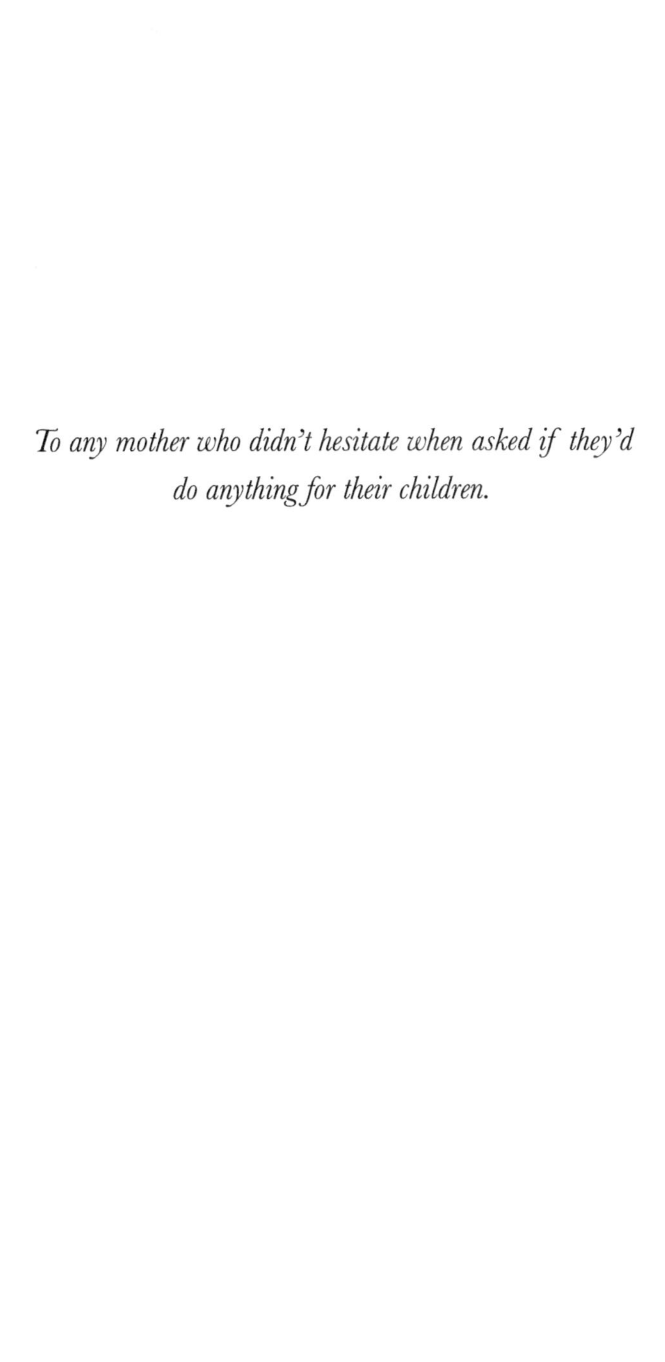

To any mother who didn't hesitate when asked if they'd do anything for their children.

CHAPTER 1

The air throughout the City of Anima hummed, as alive as the insects buzzing between the flowers dangling from vines that climbed every inch of the towering buildings. The anticipation crawled along Serena's skin, seeping beneath the surface more and more with every moment she walked through the city. Her blood rushed in response, her heart pounding so hard it threatened to leap right through her ribs.

Holding the hem of her sleeve to her nose, she drank in the calming scent of vanilla and jasmine she'd sprayed there before leaving her office.

Just a little further, she told herself. One more level up, one more footbridge, and three doors until she was home. Where her mother awaited her, her calming aura would be ready to embrace Serena and save her from the bustle of the city.

It was always worst on the streets far below, but people still milled about, even on the top levels of the city where her family lived. They hung flags, decorated their front doors, and excitedly prepared for the guard's ceremony the next day.

Her shoulders caved in, trying to avoid brushing against anyone and risking taking more than she could handle. Inwardly, she appreciated everyone's enthusiasm; she just wished they kept it to themselves.

Stepping off the footbridge that swayed slightly in the open air, Serena turned toward home. Brown-speckled finches hopped along the stone walkway, embracing the energy pouring off the Anima around them. Serena ducked beneath an overhanging branch, a lounging cat's paw swaying in the open air, lazily watching the excited birds she tried not to step on.

Two more doors and she'd be home.

The sight of her family's half-door sent a wave of relief through her, making the city's overwhelming life bearable.

Normally, she had her commute home perfectly planned to avoid as many people as possible. She had her hours at the dull paper-pushing job she'd been lucky enough to get—despite a blatant lack of magic in her veins—rearranged to accommodate her crippling social anxiety so her trek through the city was made at the least busy times of the day. But with the festival the next day, there was no avoiding it, no hiding in the slow hours of the day.

People were happy—they had every right to be—and she would be, too… if she weren't on the brink of a meltdown.

Pushing through the half-door of her apartment, a gray, yellow-beaked starling nearly scraped her cheek with its wing as it raced past.

It immediately twittered to the rest of the flock scattered throughout the room, announcing her homecoming.

Serena fell back against the wall, her knees crumpling as she held her sleeve to her nose.

Calm. She needed the calm, the soothing mix of scents she'd concocted to ease her mind and settle her spirit.

With each heartbeat, her rushing blood slowed. The wild howling of emotions pacing like a feral cat in her veins calmed with every moment she separated herself from the surrounding city. Composing herself enough to breathe, her hand fell from her face, and other scents hit her.

Cinnamon. Nutmeg. Apples. Sugar.

The sweet and spicy scent of her childhood. It reached out to her, drawing her further into the apartment and giving her the strength to stand again.

Quietly, she stepped into the kitchen, the pan on the stove confirming what she already knew. A fresh batch of her mother's apple-nut rolls, glazed with a thick coat of sweet cream frosting, tempted her closer.

Biting her lip, Serena glanced around for signs of her mother, finding only her starlings everywhere. There were always a few of them around, whether her mother was home or not, poking their head out of one of the floor-to-ceiling tree trunks littered with holes. But their presence didn't *necessarily* mean her mother was paying attention.

Sticking out a finger, ready to swipe a dollop of frosting—for comfort, of course—the starlings' twitter turned into an orchestra. Several of them franticly hopped across the branches. Side-eyeing them, Serena debated whether it was worth the risk and decided it was.

Just before her finger touched the sweet glaze, one of them swooped, and her mother's voice rang out from somewhere in the apartment. "Young lady! I know you're not about to ruin those rolls."

Slumping, Serena rolled her eyes and scowled at the group of chattering starlings. "Snitches."

"I heard that."

One of the gray birds hopped onto the closest branch, opened its bright yellow beak, and squeaked right in her face—a reprimand as effective as a finger wag. Eyes narrowing, Serena debated flicking the thing. But that would only cause more trouble. So, instead, she turned away and decided on a snack of berries.

She offered one to the wide-eyed lemur lounging in the sun on the living room windowsill. Long, deft fingers took it gratefully, nibbling away on the sweet flesh. Its tail swished through the humid air, made thick by the misters that gave the wet side of the city its name.

Absently, Serena wondered who it belonged to, if anyone. Though it was probably just hanging out until her father and his little snood monkey, Ned, got home.

"Must you piss them off already? It is far too early to listen to their complaining."

Serena's mother strode down the hallway, fingers rubbing her temple. Serena knew her mother had probably been awake just as long as she had, waking in the dark hours of the morning to start her own ceremony preparations. Despite that, Mira was a resplendent sight to behold. Shoulder-length mini twists pulled back into a clip showed off her beautiful, heart-shaped face.

It was her robe, though, that Serena ogled after. Emerald-green silk embroidered with golden thread in the abstract shapes of animals. It had been a gift from her father for her parents' fifth anniversary, and her mother still wore it every chance she got. The look was complete with a large black cockatoo the length of Serena's forearm, Rain, perched on her mother's shoulder.

The Anima woman took one look at Serena and understood the stress written across her face. Her mother cupped her cheeks, and Serena closed her eyes, absorbing the tranquil, free nature of her mother's touch. Mira emanated freedom akin to a bird floating on a breeze high above all its worries—the perfect antidote to the overwhelming thrum of the city outside.

"You're sure you want to go tomorrow?"

Serena's heart ached.

No, she didn't want to go to the guard's ceremony the next day, brushing shoulders with all those people and the cloud of emotions that came with them. But it was Seth's swearing-in ceremony, and she would never miss such an important moment in her twin's life.

She nodded, ignoring the way her stomach soured at the thought. Instead, she did her best to smile, failing to convince even herself. "I wouldn't miss it for the world."

Her mother gave her a tight-lipped smile, knowing it wasn't worth arguing. "Then let's get started, shall we?"

Serena found the book she'd selected for the day, and her mother transferred Rain from her shoulder to a nearby perch. Storm, the male cockatoo already perched there, fluffed out his feathers, eager for his paired mate to be by his side once again.

Serena read aloud over the next several hours as her mother worked on her hair. It took nearly the entire day, but by the end, her halo of naturally tight coils had turned into dozens of thin braids that ended in strands of red brushing against the middle of her back.

It hadn't been until recently that her mother started doing her hair at home again. But with each passing day, the realization that Serena and Seth would move out soon weighed on the entire household. A thick, heavy understanding shrouded every moment they had together. Serena would take any opportunity to spend more time with her mother and take in the serenity that passed through her fingers.

As afternoon turned to evening, the calm of the apartment evaporated, replaced with the energy of her father and brother, interrupting her last braid.

"There's my beautiful woman!" her father cheered when his eyes landed on her mother, his ever-present fervor for life lighting up his face. Even Ned chittered away, scampering up one of the thick ropes hanging next to the door and meeting their lemur guest in the overhanging woven hammock. Their energetic cheer immediately flooded the apartment, mixing with her mother's calm serenity to create a fog of peace Serena could practically taste.

Seth entered behind their father, rolling his feline green eyes, the exact match to her own. The long-legged spotted serval draped around his neck barely cracked her eyes to give them all a disapproving once-over before falling back asleep.

Serena did her best to ignore Ari. It had been ten years since the serval prowled the city searching for her brother, but Serena had never grown used to having the predator in the house. She swore the cat's hungry eyes watched her at all hours, day and night.

"I thought I was your favorite girl," Serena mocked, pouting as she eyed the pastry bag in her father's hand, the *Train Treats Bakery* logo stamped on the front.

"Of course. I could never forget about the second most beautiful girl in my life." Her father winked. "That's why I threw in an extra tropical twist croissant."

He kissed her mother on the temple. Storm mimicked the movement, emitting a loud smacking sound as he pressed his beak to Rain's cheek. Rain fluffed her feathers in the bird's equivalent of a blush that imitated her mother's.

Serena dug through the bag, swatting away Seth's thieving fingers when he tried to steal a bite. Croissants oozing with yellow citrus jam made from the best fruits the city offered filled the bag, and she bit into one without a second thought. The tangy, sweet notes of fruit burst across her tongue. She moaned with ecstasy, flakes of pastry covering her chin.

Her mother laughed, combing out the last section of Serena's hair to be braided. "So, hon, how was your day?"

"Fascinating!" her father enthused, pushing his glasses up the bridge of his nose. "We're still working on that cooling system for the guard that returned from the City of Kinetics and his wolverine. We've fit a private barrack with a cooling system that is substantial enough to keep them comfortable during their downtime. Still, with the barrack's proximity between the wet and dry sides of the city, it keeps gathering too much humidity and freezing."

Ari gave an annoyed sneeze, shaking her head and stretching her lean legs at the mention of the new guard.

"That guy's a creep," Seth sneered, a disgusted noise emanating from the back of his throat.

"Seth," her mother warned.

"What? He is. There's a reason he and his wolverine did so well stuck up in the mountains with the Kinetics." Seth's face flattened into an emotionless dead glare that made Serena chuckle.

Her mother swatted one of his muscle-padded shoulders half-heartedly, smiling at the —in Serena's opinion, spot-on—impression. "Knock that off."

Seth laughed, darting out of the way and stealing a piece of Serena's pastry in the process.

"Hey!"

"We do not make fun of others in this household," Mira scolded.

Everyone turned to her and raised identical eyebrows in unison.

As Director of Communications for the Anima Mother, Mira had more contact with the other cities than anyone else in the City of Anima. She also went on endless rants about the difficulty of dealing with people who hid their emotions behind masks as impenetrable as the metals they mined.

"Not. A. Word." Her mother warned, looking each of them in the eye with every word, ending with their father, who bit his lip to keep from laughing.

Serena pressed her full lips together to hold back her chuckle. Instead, she soaked in the joy and ease that swirled through the apartment and tried not to think about how different life would be that time tomorrow.

CHAPTER 2

Suffocating. The mass of people stuffing themselves into the open-air square at the city's center was suffocating. Energy rolled off them until their emotions created an acidic fog that shoved itself down her throat, seeped into her skin, and choked out what little air she gulped down.

"Focus, center. Find yourself," Mira murmured, rubbing her thumb against the back of Serena's hand.

Swallowing hard, Serena closed her eyes and turned inward.

Find yourself. Easier said than done.

Dipping her chin to her chest, she let her braids fall forward. The fine mist oils she'd sprayed on them that morning wafted a sweet and spicy scent, the closest she could get to the delectable scent of the apple-nut rolls at home.

Steady, deep breaths filled her lungs and mind with the scent, slowing her racing heart. The little reprieve it gave her made it easier to sift through all the emotions assaulting her.

Apprehension.

That wasn't hers. That was the anticipation of the guards being sworn in and fearing the worst. Of course, they would not turn down any of them that day. That wasn't what the ceremony was for. Every guard-to-be had already passed all their tests and trials. The ceremony was a day of celebration, but still, there were always a few whose imagination spiraled.

Serena's heart went out to those anxious guards and family members, but there was nothing she could do to help. Their anxiety was their own, so she pushed it away.

Focused determination with a hint of boredom—that definitely wasn't hers.

She peaked through the gaps in her braids and spotted a nearby seasoned guard on duty. He wasn't a guard-to-be like her brother, waiting to be sworn in. He was a guard who was watching for anyone looking to cause trouble.

Something about him felt… wrong. Stoic and hard, he radiated none of the warmth so common among the Anima people. Instead, he scanned the crowd with cold eyes, square jaw clenched so hard she wondered if his teeth were cracking. A slight shift in the people around her allowed her to spot the thick brown fur of a wolverine stalking the crowd's edge.

So that was the guard on loan from the Kinetic City.

His dark, red-brown eyes caught hers, and she glanced away, feeling the weight of his attention on her back.

Closing her eyes again, Serena pushed away the emotions trying to force their way into her heart.

What was *she* feeling?

Pride. Excitement. Eagerness. Love.

Seth had been training for that moment

since Ari found him ten years ago. Her parents had immediately registered the pairing with the City of Anima, an easy feat given her mother's position. One messenger bird and a couple of hours later, a guard was at their door, informing them that Seth was required to attend one year of training to ensure he could safely keep the predator in a city full of prey animals and people. He started his training the next day and never left.

Since they were eighteen, he was finally of age to be officially sworn in, and Serena couldn't be prouder.

Digging down further, she nestled herself into her own emotions. The further she sunk, the more they filled her, keeping away the over-whelming nature of emotions that weren't hers.

A horn blasted as her heart beat to its own rhythm once again, and she opened her eyes.

The crowd cheered, layered upon the sound of excited animals until the cheer became a roar. Various primates howled from over-hanging branches and netting strung up on the sides of buildings, dogs barked, birds sang, and insects of all kinds fluttered above their heads. People and animals fed off each other, creating a swirl of life that flowed like a current through the square. A current Serena had to focus to keep from being swept up in. Instead, she focused on her own rising thrill.

Through the surrounding bodies, she glimpsed the Anima Mother, striding with feline grace toward the dais in the center of the square. Just the sight of her made Serena's spirit soar.

Serena climbed onto a nearby lamppost, standing on the stone base to get a better view.

Flanked by an army of massive cats and wolves, the Anima Mother did not need the entourage of guards following close behind. Hawks and eagles with wingspans as wide as Serena's arms swooped low, nearly brushing the heads of cheering onlookers.

Reina, the current Anima Mother, commanded attention. She brought to life the very essence of power and strength—not the type a person hid from, that came with the promise of violence, but one a person ran to.

Her poise came with the assurance of safety and security, a fierce protector.

Mother Reina's black hair matched her raven skin, glowing in the midday sun. It was braided tight against her scalp in intricate patterns, ending abruptly at the crown to let her naturally tight coils halo her. But it was her eyes that stood out—absent of pupil or iris. They were entirely milky white. Despite her sightlessness, Mother Reina was not unseeing.

She was one of the most powerful Anima Mothers in history and saw *through* her animals. Rumor had it she could see through all of them at once. That she didn't have one familiar, one animal she connected with on a soul-deep level, but a dozen. All the very definitions of predator, all of them female, and all fierce protectors of the mother, her people, and her city.

Behind her was a parade of creatures and people. First, the Anima Grandmother, the previous mother who had stepped down ten years prior but still held a position of authority and respect as part of the mother's court. A forest scorpion nearly a foot long rode on the distinguished grandmother's shoulder, the perfect embodiment of the deadly tongue she was said to have.

Behind them were the daughters, the young girls still in the running to become the next heir.

The procession of women and the beasts who bowed to them climbed the stairs to the dais, greeting the mass of citizens with warm smiles and waves. A mountain lion, tawny fur burning golden in the sunlight, prowled across the stage until it found a spot on the corner to lay, massive paws hanging over the edge. A brown-feathered golden eagle that had circled the crowd swooped down and landed on the back of a chair. Every animal had its place, working in tandem with the women who commanded the people's attention.

Mother Reina crouched at the edge of the stage, meeting as many outstretched hands as she could while a dark-furred wolf that must have weighed twice the mother herself watched each movement with intensity. The brilliant woman before them radiated patience and love as she stood and waited for the roar of the masses to quiet.

"Hello, everyone. We could not have asked the Mother Above for a more perfect day for our yearly guard ceremony." Her voice rang through the square, and Serena felt her eyes mist in the mother's presence.

Lost in a world of her own emotions, Serena's heart swelled. With pride. With joy. With unbridled fearlessness. It was so rare for her to feel free and weightless, especially when surrounded by so many. But Serena felt nothing but safe when the mother's snowy eyes scanned the crowd in time with her many animal companions.

Safe to be herself. Safe to feel.

"Many of the guards being sworn in today have worked nearly their entire lives for this moment. For the chance to earn the title of city guard. But first, we must remember them by far more cherished names. Daughter. Son. Sister. Brother. Cousin. Uncle. Aunt. The titles given to them by those who love them most and those they are swearing to protect. Here in the City of

Anima, our family, both given and chosen, is what we hold above all else.

"And as is tradition, we take our lead from the animals guiding and protecting us. In the wild, it is the mothers who are the most fierce, most devoted, and most sacred. At this time, I ask anyone who has acted as a mother to step forward. From those who gave birth to the children they love to those who cared for children who weren't their own. From mothers who lost their chance to be the caregivers they dreamed of due to circumstances they could not control to those who sacrificed their chance to raise their own so their little ones had the best chance at life. Regardless of magic class, age, or circumstance, I ask you to step forward and form the way."

Women from every corner of the square started forward, moving like a million fish through water until they all converged to form a path leading to the stairs at the front of the dais. Mothers of all kinds and all magic classes lined the path on either side, shoulder to shoulder. The newly formed aisle stretched from the dais down the main street, an artery that was the lifeline of the city.

"Candidates," the mother called, her voice ringing loud and true, amplified by a Kinetic at the front of the dais, "Come forward, and remember why you serve."

The aisle stretched so far that it took several minutes before Serena glimpsed the guard candidates. At the front was Eva, Seth's second, leading the pack of chest-swollen guards-to-be. As the candidates passed, the mothers lining their path reached out, their fingertips skimming the candidate's shoulders, arms, and hands. Barely a whisper of skin on skin, but with each step, one touch became hundreds. It was a symbolic moment where the mothers imbued the candidates with strength and responsibility. The line of mothers reminded the pack who they served and why; they also bestowed the candidates a piece of their heart —a transfer of trust from one protector to another.

As the leader, Seth brought up the rear, Ari prowling at his side.

At the sight of him, Serena couldn't contain her overwhelming elation. It filled her eyes with tears and made her blood pound in her ears. It poured out of her as if she couldn't contain the emotions, and she swore the people around her fed the energy back to her. A constant ebb and flow that made her corner of the square cheer the loudest. She threw her head back and howled, laughing as the weight of her earlier suffocation left her. As if a million hands were taking just an ounce of her stress until there was nothing left but happiness.

As the candidates climbed the stairs to the dais, they kneeled, one by one, before Mother Reina. In turn, she placed her hands on their shoulders. An intimately tender moment where both closed their eyes, a sign of complete trust, and their familiars—if the guard had one—mingled.

Most Anima connected with a singular animal, finding at least one familiar in their lives, no matter how little magic they had. Such was her father and his snood monkey, Ned. But some connected to whole sects of animals instead. Such as her mother, who could connect with any bird but mostly connected with starlings and found a familiar in Rain.

When the guard's familiar or chosen companion for the day was looked over by every familiar on the stage and deemed worthy, the guard stood and moved to the side so the next could perform the ceremony.

Seth was the last to kneel before the mother.

As the strongest of the group and their chosen leader, it was his job to look after them all. In the ceremony, his last place was symbolic, but in practice, it would be his responsibility to not only lead the group but join them. A true leader didn't sit back and watch as those below them rode headfirst into danger. He would watch their backs, be the last to come home, and never leave a fellow sister or brother behind.

As Seth kneeled, Ari prowled among the familiars, touching noses with some and rubbing against others. Sometimes, she would sit back and wait for the familiar to approach her, such as when the golden eagle watched her for several moments before singing its approval.

The mingling of familiars and companions wasn't just symbolic, either. It was a show of power as much as submission. Seth's ability to keep Ari calm in the chaos of the ceremony and mingle amongst so many predators and prey in a way that wasn't natural for her was a feat beyond words.

When Seth's moment with the mother was over, he rose and found his place at the end of the line of newly sworn-in guards along the front of the dais.

Mother Reina stood at the center and raised her hands above her head. "May I present to you, the children of the Mother Above, your newest protectors. Welcome them as you would your own."

The crowd roared, and the cheering, clapping, howling, and barking nearly shook the towering buildings. People and animals alike rejoiced as every beast on the stage rose and descended into the crowd, Ari among their ranks.

Serena whooped and shrieked in tandem with those around her, letting every emotion building within her flow out and into others. She imagined her heart as a breaking dam, bursting with emotion until she couldn't contain it. She blanketed the throng with her joy, covering it with cheer, happiness, pride, and love.

CHAPTER 3

Finally, the celebration ebbed, and Serena climbed down from her perch, feeling as light as one of her mother's birds.

Her father clapped her on the shoulder, filling her with another wave of life. "They did great, didn't they?"

"It couldn't have gone better."

The man who raised Serena, who looked upon his wife and children with enough warmth to fuel a wildfire, wrapped his arms around her shoulders and kissed the top of her head. In moments like those, he often forgot she didn't like to be touched. Too often, people carried something dark beneath their mask of light, and Serena could feel every shadowed layer of it, even in her ever-jovial father. But that day… that day, there was room for nothing but happiness.

Out of the corner of her eye, Serena caught sight of the guard with the wolverine speaking urgently with Mother Reina at the edge of the stage. Serena forced herself to look away from the stoic guard, whose eyes had felt so wrong when they landed on her.

It wasn't until her father's brows furrowed and something more urgent than curiosity flowed through his touch that she followed her father's gaze.

She pulled out of his arms, doing everything to disconnect herself from the sudden negativity.

"Dad? What's going on?"

Guards converged on the dais, urgently speaking among themselves and the mother. Seth and his fellow new guards didn't budge from their rigid stand of attention. It was a day to show their control over themselves and their animal bonds. But the other guards all whispered as they scanned the people, gazes jumping from one face to another.

"I… I don't know. I'm sure it's nothing." Her father stumbled over the words, and Serena tasted his uncertainty like a sour fruit.

Birds flittered over the crowd, swooping and frantically singing to anyone who would listen. A handful of Anima perked up at their call, including her mother across the crowd. Her heart-shaped face fell as she spun, looking for something.

An uneasy air rippled through the crowd as more and more people sensed the shift in the guards and the mother. Even Ned chattered on her father's shoulder, frantically pawing at her father's shaven head.

"Dad…" Serena started, unsure what to ask. She didn't have a speck of magic and couldn't tell what messages were passing through the creatures. But he could.

Her father turned his spectacled gaze to her,

and his growing panic slammed against her, practically throwing her back a step.

The world spun as too many bodies became frantic, their fear and growing unease pressing against her. The previously spacious square became too small, the buildings closing in on her until she could barely breathe, once again suffocating her.

Serena bowed her head, palms pressing against her temples, trying to hold the pieces of herself together.

"We need to go. Now."

Her father's words barely registered, but when his fingers wrapped around her arm, insistently pulling her away, she felt his confusion, horror, and disbelief like a poison. It choked her until she couldn't breathe, and her heart constricted until she thought it might burst.

Shrieking, Serena yanked herself from his grasp. She couldn't handle the physical contact. It was all too much.

Stumbling over her feet, she tried to find a part in the crowd. Tried to find an escape. While no one else reached out to her, they also didn't give her a way out. They trapped her in a prison of their terror, and it threatened to drive her mad.

It was the vicious snarling that stopped everything.

A wolverine, hackles raised, flesh-tearing teeth bared, snarled at her.

Serena's mind fogged with her own terror, and she stared into those hateful, beady eyes. People around her whirled with alarm, running in every direction away from her and the beast.

Mouth dry, there was only one word she could whisper. "Dad?"

Her father watched the snarling predator, hands outstretched like that would keep the thing at bay. His features stayed neutral, but his wide eyes and quick breath betrayed him as much as Ned on his shoulder screeching at the wolverine. "Don't move, baby girl. It'll be ok." The words were low and soothing but laced with his true panic.

Serena couldn't even bring herself to ask what was going on. Perhaps the guard returning from the Kinetic City had lost control of his familiar, unused to so much chaos after all those years in the mountains. But the wolverine wasn't attacking. Had the guard lost control, Serena expected it would have already torn her to bloody shreds.

Then hands yanked her arms, and so many emotions crashed against her she could do nothing to fight the contact. She became power-less in the face of so many contradicting feelings from so many people.

The world spun so fast Serena vomited up what little breakfast she'd forced down that morning. Still, the hands didn't let go. Their overwhelming emotions clashed against her own with such violence that it didn't take long before Serena's world went black.

THE BUMPING and jerking of the prison carriage they'd thrown her inside woke Serena from blissful unconsciousness. The short ride ended abruptly at the entrance to the Anima Mother's estate. Guards yanked open the doors and escorted her through the halls, flanked by their animal companions. None of them so much as looked her way as she begged for an explanation and pleaded her ignorant innocence.

Cold, brutal hatred radiated from them all, mixed with the occasional twinge of fear or uncertainty whenever she begged. Eventually, she gave up her questioning, opting to walk in silence, focusing instead on the splatter of vomit on the toe of her shoes.

At least they weren't touching her anymore, though she wasn't sure if that was for her sake or their own. For some reason, she sensed when she got whiffs of that fear; it was fear of *her*.

She tried to dismiss it. What city guard would fear an eighteen-year-old girl who worked in an office and didn't possess a grain of magic? But no matter how hard she worked to convince herself she was a threat to no one, she couldn't shake the feeling the guards were giving her an extra wide berth.

Finally, they entered what could only be described as an indoor jungle. Plants and trees of every kind filled every corner, leaving only a stone pathway over a small babbling creek. The path led to a circular sitting area filled with a council of women. The Anima Grandmother and Daughters all sat in small, cushioned chairs flanking a metaphorical throne at the center, upon which sat Mother Reina, still clad in her celebratory garb.

The city guards shoved Serena to her knees before the council. She fell to the ground, shaky legs giving out beneath her. Hunched forward, she dared to glance up through her braids and meet the solid white eyes of the Anima Mother. The weight of dozens of eyes bore down on her, both human and animal, as the council and their familiars watched her. It took every bit of willpower she possessed not to whimper in the face of such beauty and power.

Mother Reina's voice was sharp as a lion's bite when she spoke, her words losing every bit of love and patience they had harbored during her earlier speech. "Serena Aviacer, you stand accused of being a Mind-Bender. How do you plead?"

Serena's mouth fell open, but no words

came out.

As a child growing up without magic, she'd been called many things, but Mind Bender had never been one of them.

Shaking her head, she struggled to hold herself together beneath the crushing weight of so many bodies emanating such strong emotions. "I… No, I… Mind Bender… But I don't have any magic." Her throat constricted, and the tears threatening to fall streaked her shaking words.

The Anima Mother lifted a beckoning hand. A guard stepped forward, sparing Serena a hateful glance, before bowing his head to the mother.

The guard from the Kinetic City.

"Whit claims to have felt the manipulative touch of a Mind Bender's magic coming from you during the guard's ceremony. Being sensitive to emotions after so long among the stoic Kinetics, I have every reason to believe his claim."

"But I don't have any magic!" Serena cried. There was nothing else for her to say. How could she possibly prove she *didn't* possess something? If she had magic, she could show them—show them her animal companion, show them how she could call insects, horses, or pigs to her side. But she couldn't demonstrate a *lack* of magic.

"Lying manipulative bitch," Whit snapped, not even a hair of sympathy lacing the disgust he wielded.

Serena shrunk beneath his hateful words, feeling the strike like it was tangible.

"See?" Whit pointed, his wolverine at his heel taking a snarling step toward her. "She flinches because she can tell what I'm thinking. What we're all thinking. The perfect act."

Undiluted panic of Serena's own making flooded her as she looked into that wolverine's beady eyes. She fell back on her hands, ready to crawl if it meant putting distance between herself and the brown-haired demon.

"Enough!" the mother snapped, pulling Serena's attention. "Whit, I understand that during your time with the Kinetics, you grew accustomed to their dulled ways and that rejoining the Anima people has been over-whelming. However, I will happily send you back to training if you cannot control your familiar. Am I understood?" Her icy eyes narrowed on the guard, and several deadly-looking animals pushed to their feet by her side, preparing to step in if necessary.

Whit swallowed hard, shifting his hard gaze to the ground to regain control. The wolverine at his feet stilled, falling back against his legs, though its hackles remained raised.

"Very good." Mother Reina and the hawk at her shoulder turned their attention to Serena, her other familiars keeping one eye on the bristling wolverine. "I suppose there is only one way to settle this."

The mother stood, but the grandmother placed a hand on her shoulder, sensing what she was about to do. "My daughter, don't be so proud that you risk yourself. If this girl truly is a Mind-Bender…"

"If she is truly a Dark Magic wielder," the mother started, her voice ringing loud through the room, "Then may the Mother Above command my familiars to end my tainted mind."

The daughters' eyes widened, understanding and horror rolling off them in violent waves as they finally grasped the mother's intentions. A mountain cat and wolf flanked the mother as she approached, moving as gracefully as the predators at her sides.

Serena trembled, her shaking muscles threatening to rattle right off her bones as the mother stepped closer. Looming above her hunched form, Reina held out a dark hand.

Serena simply stared at the offering, unable to bring herself to bridge the gap between herself and the mother.

"Serena." Her name rolled off the mother's tongue as both a warning and a command.

Stomach twisting, Serena lifted a trembling hand. She hesitated, letting it hang in mid-air as she met the mother's sightless white eyes. The entire room tensed, poised to separate the two at the mother's first signal.

Tears streaked Serena's face, salting her lips with her fear.

"Please," she begged quietly. "I don't know what I did."

Mother Reina's strong face softened just a hair. Enough that it reminded Serena of the protective strength she'd emanated during the ceremony. "Then prove yourself."

Bowing her head, Serena placed her fingertips against the mother's palm.

Gasping so hard it knocked the air from her lungs, sensation—not only the mother's but those of a dozen different animals—pummeled Serena.

Hatred. Tension. Fear. Anger. Wariness. Trepidation. Hunger for flesh.

So many emotions that they pummeled her, washing over her with wave after wave of heart-pounding adrenaline. She didn't know how the mother could stand it, being in not only her own body but that of a dozen different predators. That she hadn't spiraled into madness was a wonder in itself. It took everything Serena had to keep her head above the waves and fight the ripping undertow from dragging her into the depths of those emotions.

Roaring blood filled her ears, her own panic warring with everything being forced into her.

Mind Bender. Mind Bender. Mind Bender.

The title pierced her over and over again, goading her panic until it was a full-blown attack. The life force flowing from her fingers to the mother's palm shifted, and suddenly, the mother's emotions weren't assaulting her any longer. Instead, Serena's own emotions leached out of her, pushing through her fingers and into the mother's hand.

The moment of the shift, the mother hissed, yanking her hand away like Serena's finger burned.

The grandmother and daughters all shot to their feet. The predators surrounding the room jumped to attention. Some stepped out of the foliage, converging closer and closer. Serena feared that one wrong move, and they'd tear her to bloody ribbons.

But she couldn't stop it. Her building fear continued to flow out of her. It filled every inch of the room like a fog, spreading until it touched each person one by one. They all took a step back in turn, trying to distance them- selves from her and the overwhelming horror she exuded. Wrapping her arms around herself, she tried to hold the pieces of herself together, as if she could pull the panic back inside and stop how it leaked from her every pore.

Silent moments turned to tension-filled minutes as every one of them watched her. Their disgust was a sticky syrup on her tongue.

Peeking up from beneath her lashes, Serena watched the mother, tears dripping to the stone floor.

"Daughter…" the grandmother whispered, fiercely concerned.

"I'm fine," the mother replied, but a slight tremble to her words betrayed how thoroughly Serena had shaken her. "Morning. We will execute her at daybreak."

"No!" Serena shrieked, but no one paid her any attention. The tears came quicker, flowing in streams down her face and staining the collar of her shirt. "Please! It's not Dark Magic. I'm not a Mind Bender. I don't know what this is, but it's not that. I can't read minds; I can't manipulate them!"

"You just did," Reina spoke quietly, but it didn't weaken her words. In fact, Serena sensed a hint of sympathy in her voice, but she knew that small mercy wouldn't save her.

"Why not do it now, Mother?" The eldest of the daughters asked, her long locs flowing over her shoulders, as thick as the snake wrapped around her arm from wrist to shoulder.

"Today is a day of celebration. We will give her family time to say their goodbye, then we will put an end to this."

Despair wrapped itself around Serena's heart and squeezed so hard she could feel it tearing at the seams.

The Anima Mother flicked her fingers. "Take her away."

The grandmother and daughters flocked to Reina's side as city guards converged around Serena, blocking the mother from view. They herded her from the room, ignoring her sobs and pleas, ending any chance she had for mercy.

CHAPTER 4

Serena had never found comfort nor torment in darkness. She'd never been afraid of shadows and had even grown fond of them as she got older, if only because the dark meant fewer people to contend with. But sitting on the cold stones of her cell, surrounded by nothing but blackness, it felt like the darkness was alive. It counted her every remaining heartbeat with an air of malice.

It wasn't until the staccato of several sets of footsteps broke the silence that she realized she'd been listening to the sound of her own breath to stave off the quiet.

The Anima cells had various types of doors for various types of prisoners, and Serena's was solid metal. She couldn't see her mother coming down the hall, but she could certainly hear her.

"Where is she? Where is my daughter?"

Serena scrambled to her feet when her cell door creaked open. A starling rushed in first, followed closely by her mother the moment she could fit through the crack. Both her father and Seth followed close behind, the four of them filling every corner of the small cell.

Mira wrapped her arms around Serena, nearly bowling her daughter over. Serena allowed herself only a moment in her mother's arms before stepping out of them and holding her mother at arm's length.

"No, don't come any closer," she pled quietly. "I don't want them to think I've manipulated you."

"Baby girl," her father said quietly, the way he used to when she was young and having a nightmare, "We're not afraid of you."

Serena sniffed. "But the mother…"

"The mother," Mira cut in, the title harsh

on her tongue in a way Serena had never heard before, "May be the mother of our people, but she is not *your* mother. I carried you, bore you, and have spent every single day of the last eighteen years raising you. I don't care what they say. You are not Dark."

Serena felt confidence and a protective air roll off her mother, filling the small cell. It wrapped around her, tucking her in and comforting her like a bedtime story.

A sob wrenched through Serena's chest, and her lips trembled, making her whispered words shake. "They're going to kill me. I don't even know what I did."

"You manipulated people," Seth stated so matter-of-factly that Serena flinched.

"Seth," her father hissed.

"What? My sister's twelve hours away from execution, and you want me to beat around the bush? That's what they're accusing her of."

"Keep your voice down," her mother scolded.

"Ari is right outside, keeping watch, but no one will hear. No other guards want to come anywhere near this cell. They think she's going to control them through the damned door." Seth threw his hands up, running one over the short, thick locs atop his head and shorn sides.

"Your sister does *not* have Dark Magic," her father growled.

Serena shrunk at the sound. She didn't even know her father could make such a noise.

"I'm not saying she does, but we've all been there when she's gotten overwhelmed. We've all felt… *it*. Whatever *it* is."

Her parents locked eyes, a silent conversation passing between them before turning to Serena in unison.

She stared down at her hands, searching the lines etched into her palms for answers. *Mind Bender…*

Her father's voice was full of hard confidence when he said her name. "Serena," he started, "You're my baby girl, and I trust your word above all others. If you tell us you aren't a Mind Bender, then I will believe you until my last breath, but I need you to say it."

At that moment, Serena saw only her father

—not the man who obsessed over heating and cooling systems and could spend endless hours debating the newest building materials.

No, he was her *father.* The man who rocked her to sleep and whispered bedtime stories when she wouldn't stop crying from colic. The man who moved spiders that had wandered into her room while telling her that all the Mother Above's creatures deserved to live, but that didn't mean they had to live next to her bed. Who had taught her to hold her head high when the kids at school taunted her lack of magic.

"How would I even know?" Serena squeaked.

Eyebrows furrowing, he let out a heavy sigh through his nose. He studied her momentarily, trying to find a response and eventually landing on, "Do you remember what I told you when you were six and asked how to tell if a bunny was your familiar or just *really* cute?"

Through her tears, the corner of Serena's lip lifted into a sad smile. "You said to follow my heart."

"Because…"

She sighed, her shoulders falling. "You said, 'Hearts are our guides. Listen, and you'll never be lost.' "

Her father gave her a small, sad smile of his own, and she felt his nostalgia as heavily as a hug. "Exactly, baby girl. You'll know."

Serena closed her eyes with one last long sigh, breathing the way her mother had taught her. *Find yourself*, she'd say. If only Serena had known that one day, those words wouldn't just refer to navigating a jungle of emotions to find her own heart buried somewhere in the center.

Find yourself. Hearts are our guides: listen, and you'll never be lost.

Dipping her chin to her chest, she cataloged all the emotions crowding the cell—her mother's patience, her brother's determination, and her father's certainty—she pushed them all away until she could truly focus on the beating of her own heart. It pounded against her breastbone in a steady rhythm, but no matter how hard she listened, it didn't speak to her.

Cautiously, Serena allowed herself to turn

the title of Mind Bender over in her thoughts. She held it there, cradling it in the palm of her mind, testing its weight. Instinctively, raw fear and unease reared at its presence, at the reputation such a title wielded.

Biting her lip, Serena forced herself to ignore that fear. How could she ask her heart to accept the title if she was so focused on her negative association with it? She needed to be as objective as possible.

So she took that title that felt so heavy in her mind's hands and placed it on a shelf alongside every other magic class. She lined it up perfectly next to Shifter, Elemental, Witch, Kinetic, and Anima. But no matter how she studied it, straightened it, and rearranged it, the title of Mind Bender just felt... wrong. Her heart rejected it with a vengeance, constricting at just the thought of putting that label on herself.

Serena tested each of those titles, and each made her heart twinge in its own unique way. But when she got to Anima, it sighed contentedly. Her heart wore the magic class like a medal, proudly proclaiming who she was to her core.

When Serena opened her eyes again, her hands didn't shake, and her lip no longer trembled. "No, I'm not a Mind Bender. I'm an Anima. I just… don't understand how."

"All Anima are sensitive to emotions; that's how we communicate with our animals. I always assumed you were just broken," Seth offered.

Serena narrowed her green eyes at her twin, hoping he saw how unhelpful he was being.

"Your sister is not broken," her mother scolded. "Just like you are not broken for having a predator familiar."

Seth threw up his hands in defense, his sleeveless uniform showing off the muscles he'd built from so many years of training. "Some people would argue that too, just saying. Lots of Anima insist the familiar reflects the Anima, which would make me as dangerous as Ari." When her mother reverted her gaze in resignation of the common belief, he lowered his hands and muttered under his breath, "Ask any guard, though; people are way scarier than animals."

"People *are* animals," her father chimed in, her family falling into a familiar banter. "That's what makes them so dangerous."

People are animals... Serena turned the words over in her mind until they settled in her heart, right alongside her title of Anima.

"People are animals," Serena repeated, her words no louder than a whisper. Looking up, she met the gaze of her mother, father, and, lastly, her brother. Staring into a reflection of her own feline green eyes, her own soul, she repeated the realization. And the words sunk into her like a warm meal on a cold night. "People are animals."

Her parents exchanged another glance, but Serena couldn't tear her eyes from Seth as they shared a conversation all their own. She felt as much as saw the exact moment he understood.

Shaking her head, her mother looked at Serena warily out of the corner of her eye. "I'm sorry, baby girl, but we don't know what you mean."

"People are animals," Seth repeated, lifting his hand in an offering, palm out to Serena.

For the first time since Serena could remember, she reached out and willingly met her brother's palm with her own. Her long, slender fingers were nearly as long as his thick ones, stretching along his calloused palm.

For her entire life, Serena had avoided touching anyone. The utter onslaught of emotions it invited threatened to consume her, to pull her beneath cresting waves crashing against her until she spiraled into the depths of her mind.

But finally, she understood.

When the emotions hit, she didn't shy away from them. After a beat of hesitation, Serena welcomed the flow of energy emanating from her brother. She drank in his trust and understanding, the faith in one another that only came from spending every moment of your life with someone. Words weren't necessary between them because she *felt* everything, every beat of his heart and breath, working in time with her own.

Seth didn't fear her. He never would. Just as she trusted him to control Ari, he trusted her with his heart.

"I am an Anima," Serena proclaimed to her small family. "Anima magic is all about emotion, and people are animals."

"Is that even possible?" her father asked, and when Serena looked at him, she saw the wheels in his never-resting mind reeling faster than a hummingbird's wings.

"I don't know," her mother breathed, teeth worrying along her bottom lip. "But if it is, we must speak with Mother Reina immediately."

"She's never going to believe us." Seth's voice edged toward anger, but Serena felt the underlying refusal to accept reality fueling it.

"Then we'll just have to make her listen," her mother declared, as if it were that easy. "I'm getting you out of here, baby girl, one way or another."

Tears swam along Serena's lashes as she took in her mother's face, forcing herself to memorize every detail. She didn't doubt her mother would talk to Mother Reina, but no matter how hard she searched the cell, Serena couldn't find a speck of honest hope floating in the air. None of them genuinely believed Serena would see the day after tomorrow. Beneath all her mother's determination, there was nothing but a deep, dark layer of dread.

"I love you," Serena whispered, taking in all of them one last time. She gave both her parents and her brother a hug, briefly crushing them against her, doing her best to ignore the overwhelming grief they all pushed into her. And when they slipped out the door, shutting it with a grating groan behind them, they cut off every ray of light and hope from Serena's cell.

CHAPTER 5

It was impossible to tell how many monotonous hours passed in the blackness. No one brought her food or water. She wouldn't starve to death before her execution, so what was the point in risking a guard's safety to feed her?

After her family had left, Serena felt her way to a corner and sank to the floor. Pulling her knees to her chest, she sat… and sat… and sat… Every now and then, she would hold her fingers to her eyelids and blink just to check if her eyes were open or closed.

In a cell utterly devoid of human life,

Serena realized how empty she felt without it. She'd always dreaded being around others and dealing with the onslaught of feelings another's presence brought. But in the absence of life, she realized how dearly she needed that contact.

She was an Anima, an Anima with weird, unnatural, but powerful magic that thrived on closeness. And, in the absence of all life, she felt… hollow. A shell of the person she usually was. As if someone had come and sucked it all away. As if it was the life of others that kept her own flame burning.

What Serena *did* know was that too much time had passed. Hours must have come and gone, and no one freed her. If her family was going to convince Mother Reina to spare her, they would have come for her by then. Whether it was midnight or sunrise, it made no difference: Serena was bound for execution, and she would never see her family again.

So when the subtle echo of voices grew in the corridor outside her cell, Serena almost convinced herself she'd already fallen into a loop of insanity. Dismissing the sound, she restarted her counting, unable to believe anyone would come for her.

But then… the voices stopped outside her cell door.

"Yes, Whit, I'm sure. Head back to your post."

Serena nearly wept at the familiar voice, scrambling to her feet.

Seth. Seth had come for her.

The cell door groaned open, letting in enough light for her to make out Seth's features. His short locs, his guard's uniform, and…

"Where's Ari?" she asked. Serena was so used to seeing the serval draped around his neck that her absence was alarming. Seth didn't answer but stood in the doorway, watching her. "What's going on? Did Mom convince the mother?"

Seth's gaze fell to the floor, and Serena knew.

Shaking, she wrapped her arms around herself, holding back a sob. "No… no, I'm not ready."

When her brother spoke, his eyes met hers,

but his words seemed directed elsewhere. For the benefit of another. "Please don't make this harder than it needs to be. It took everything for Mom to convince the mother to allow me to escort you."

Serena's brows furrowed at Seth's mechanical tone, like he'd chosen the words carefully and practiced them several times. He lifted a finger to his lips and held out his hand, beckoning her to take it. Uncertainty wrapped itself around Serena's chest. No matter how much she trusted her brother, she was terrified to meet his fingers. Old habits died hard, and the thought of being willing to touch someone who wasn't her mom made her want to recoil.

When his fingers wrapped around hers, the overwhelming sensation of fearless determination and selflessness that met her confused Serena. She'd been expecting anger, regret, and grief. All the things expected of a brother escorting his sister to her death. But she found none of them.

"Seth, what's…" she started, but he cut her off.

"Come on. It's time to get you out of here," he called again, and Serena got the sense those words held a double meaning she didn't yet understand.

Seth pulled her into the dimly lit corridor and silently guided her away from the cell. A high-pitched snarl emanated from the direction they headed, followed by a deeper growl that made the hairs on the back of Serena's neck stand on end.

She froze, just as she had when she heard it the last time, a lifetime ago, in the city square.

"Seth," she squeaked, "Where is Ari?"

Her brother's grip tightened on her hand, every muscle in his body coiling like overtaught springs.

"Hey! Come get your damn cat! She's gone insane," a cold voice yelled from the direction of the growing snarls. Whit's irritation radiated from the end of the hall, and Serena heard him mumbling something to the growling animals.

A momentarily pained expression passed over Seth's face, and through their clenched hands, Serena felt his heart crack. A fracture that speared his center and nearly broke him to pieces.

Chaos broke out from the end of the corridor as snarls turned to screeches and high-pitched animalistic cries.

"What in the name of the Mother Above is wrong with you! Get off!" Whit roared, pain like it was his own, lacing each word.

The fight between serval and wolverine grew to a wailing crescendo in the distance, high-pitched shrieks and battle cries ricocheting off the stone walls. Serena yanked against her brother's hold, but no matter how much his heart shattered, he didn't budge.

"What are you doing? Ari needs you!" Serena cried, not caring who heard. She thrashed against his hold until their eyes met, and she saw the silver tears along his lashes and felt the resignation weighing him down.

After a moment, the fight ended, but the snarls didn't die. Scampering paws and scratching claws scurried into the distance, followed closely by the heavy fall of boots.

The moment Whit's footsteps faded out of

earshot, Seth burst into movement. He pulled Serena after him into the dimly lit hallway, clutching her hand like it was a lifeline tethering him to the earth. She stumbled to keep up, legs and feet still tingling from so many hours curled up in the corner of her cell.

When they came to a *T* in the hallway, Serena prepared herself to go left, down the hallway lit at regular intervals, the direction still echoing with the sound of brawling, back the way the guards had brought her earlier.

But Seth pulled her to the right, in the direction shrouded in darkness.

"Where are we going? What's going on? What about Ari?" Serena babbled, so many questions pouring out of her that she couldn't tell where one stopped and where the next started. Her confusion was a tornado in her thoughts, throwing out questions with such aggressive speed she couldn't catch them before they fell out of her mouth.

Seth pulled her to an abrupt stop in the darkness. "Serena, I love you, but you need to shut up so I can save your life. Ari is… she's fine." He forced the last words through gritted teeth.

Through the energy that flowed from his fingers to hers, Serena felt how every scratch and bite against Ari pained Seth. The wolverine's claws scraped against him in phantom wounds, and she knew that Seth's heart would stop cold in his chest the moment Ari's stopped in hers.

Together, the twins ran hand in hand through the darkness in silence. The only sound came from their labored breaths and uncertain footsteps. Seth guided them down one corridor after another, and while Serena couldn't see the walls around her, she felt the way the stones beneath her feet changed, turning from smooth and well-worn to jagged and cracked. Beneath his heavy breaths, she swore Seth chanted to himself, repeating the same words over and over again. Like he might forget them if he didn't say them like a prayer.

After endless turns through the dark, he pulled them to a stop.

"Feel around; there should be a… here!"

Seth guided her hand through the dark until her fingers wrapped around a metal bar. With a large hand, he pushed against her back, guiding her… up.

"Climb. There will be a door at the top. Knock." The words left him in a rush, not wasting even a single precious moment.

"Aren't you coming with me?"

In the dark, Serena couldn't see her own eyes looking back at her or Seth's solid jaw. But the loaded hesitation and audible swallow told her everything she needed to know.

She threw her arms around her brother's neck and pulled him against her. Thick fingers dug into her back, holding her tight in a last desperate embrace.

So rarely in her life had she ever hugged her brother, and in that moment, she regretted every day she hadn't. She regretted all the times they fought and bickered and all the times she warily avoided him because Ari made her uncomfortable.

All too soon, he pulled away, pushing her toward the ladder.

"Remember, knock." Seth's voice came out choked, and Serena wasn't sure which heartbreak it stemmed from: her leaving or his familiar's sacrifice. But she could tell the serval was still fighting, still alive. Seth felt her pain digging into every inch of his skin, which meant there was still pain to feel.

"Go save Ari," she breathed and started climbing.

It was slow going in the dark, and Serena had to feel her way along every rung. By the time her fingers ran out of bars to grab, finally finding where the wall met the ceiling, her legs and arms were burning. Despite how difficult the utter black made her climb, she was thankful she couldn't see how far she would fall if she slipped.

With a single hand, she felt along the ceiling, found where stone turned to metal, and struck it with the flat of her palm as hard as she could. Once. Twice.

Immediately, something scraped above her, and the door yanked open. The sudden light of early morning blinded her, only partially blocked out by a silhouette looming over the hole above her head. Hands gripped her arms, hauling her out of her hole and ushering her into a whole other world.

"We have to hurry; the train is leaving soon," the words barely registered to her still-spinning mind, but the familiar voice nearly had Serena weeping on her knees.

"Dad?"

"It's me, I'm here," his warm voice assured her. Wrapping an arm around her shoulders, he helped her to her feet as the world came back into view around her.

Each step he led her down the unassuming alley was an effort of will, and it took everything in her power not to melt beneath his crushing mixture of love and anxiety. Ned scurried along the ground, weaving between their feet until he scampered up her father's legs and arm and perched on his shoulder.

It wasn't until they turned onto the street and wove between pedestrians that her father's words sank in.

The train is leaving soon.

Taking in her surroundings for the first time, Serena finally understood where she was.

An array of windows across the street gave shoppers a glimpse of various goods, including a selection of pastries. Nestled among the options was a flaky twist oozing with citrus jam she had enjoyed a mere two days prior. The words *Train Treats Bakery* were carved into a wooden sign hanging above the door.

An influx of people poured out of the train station, and Serena had to twist and turn between them to avoid being jostled. It took all her concentration to keep herself calm and avoid being pulverized by all the buzzing, bustling energy around her. It made the blood in her veins fizz and her thoughts whirl, blurring the world around her until the people were mere smudges in her vision.

Staring at her feet, she thought of nothing but her next step until a starling whipped around her head close enough for its wings to brush against her cheek. Moments later, a comforting, calm touch found her hand, slowing the world back to a normal pace.

"Just breathe, baby girl."

Serena found her mother's gaze and lost herself in it, letting the bustling world melt away around them.

"What's going on? What's happening?" Serena pled, desperate for answers.

Silver tears danced along her mother's lashes as her palms cupped Serena's face. Her mother studied her face, memorizing every last detail as she tucked a single braid behind her ear.

Grief and devastated acceptance clawed at Serena's throat, forcing her to see what she didn't want to acknowledge. It silenced the train's booming horn and slowed the packed platform, passengers coming and going, swirling around them as if the small family were a boulder in a stream of fish.

"I am so proud to be your mother. Stay safe, and always follow your heart." Her mother's words were streaked with sorrow, making them uneven despite how hard she tried to be strong. She slipped a ticket into one of Serena's hands and the woven strap of a bag into the other.

Serena dropped the bag to the concrete and pulled her mother into a crushing embrace.

"I'm scared," she whispered, face crumpling as she held back body-wrenching sobs.

"It's ok to be afraid. So long as you live."

A commanding voice rang out over the crowd, announcing passengers' last chance to board the train headed to the City of Elementals. Serena's heart leaped in her chest, racing as fear coursed through her veins.

"Why the Elementals? What do I do when I get there?" she sputtered.

"There are rumors that Lord Kevah is lenient toward those with Dark Magic. Stay hidden and learn how to control your magic. You'll be ok." Her mother nodded at her, and Serena mimicked the movement, though she wasn't convinced.

Before Serena knew it, the bag was once again shoved into her hands as her parents pushed her toward the train. Without thinking, she hurried up the steps and navigated down the center aisle until she found an empty row where she could nestle herself into the corner.

Staring out the window, she watched her father wrap his arms around her mother's shoulders, holding her tight. They both smiled sadly at her, tears streaking their cheeks. Ned stood on her father's shoulder and waved a small hand, swaying back and forth with the effort.

Serena placed her palm against the glass of the window, a last goodbye to both her family and the life she knew. The window made the physical distance between her and her parents feel ten times further, and her despair at their looming absence in her life poured out of her, making the air in the train car dense with grief.

When the train pulled away, the last tethers to life as she knew it snapped. The recoil of it cracked at her heart, shattering it into a million tiny shards that shredded her insides. Even the man in front of her gasped as her pain leached into him.

Serena knew she had to get herself under control. To pull herself together and reel back in all the heartache she was sending into the world. But she couldn't bring herself to care.

She clutched her bag to her chest like it could shield her from reality, using the canvas and cotton as a buffer to ward off the coming days. Silently, she cried, hiding her tears behind her braids. But when her sniffles drew concerned glances from the few other passengers in her car, she turned away and started searching the bag for something to wipe away her tears.

Her fingers wrapped around a small glass bottle rolling at the bottom, hidden beneath various pieces of clothing she didn't bother to discern. She used the mister to spray a single spritz against her sleeve and was immediately overtaken by the spicy-sweet scent of home.

CHAPTER 6

Seth

A spotted heap of bloody fur laid in a ball between Seth's feet as he stood at attention before Mother Reina's council. He barely dared to breathe beneath the grandmother's penetrating stare, using every ounce of focus to track Ari's life force. Every second she still breathed was another second he could stay standing.

She had walked away from her brush with Whit's wolverine in rough shape, but she was alive, and that's all he could hope for. They had granted him just enough time to make sure none of her wounds would cause her to bleed out right there on the floor, but it wasn't enough. The moment they dismissed him, he'd scoop her up in his arms and rush her to the nearest Witch with an affinity for animals.

The doors opened behind him, but he didn't dare break his guard's stance to see who entered. No one spoke as several sets of footsteps approached, thudding against the stone floor.

Seth risked a glance out of the corner of his eye and found his mother by his side and his father beside her. The three of them exchanged a loaded look, but none spoke. His father fidgeted, Ned pawing at his shaved head, neither of them able to sit still. His mother, however, stood perfectly poised, with Rain on her shoulder.

The silence stretched on for a lifetime, the only sound in the room heavy breathing and the occasional low growl or sigh from one of the familiars.

The tension was only broken when the

doors to the council room slammed open, and a rush of sharp-beaked birds swooped past him.

"Where is she!" Mother Reina boomed, sweeping through the room with her mountain lion and wolf at her heels.

Seth's spine became ramrod straight as he fought every instinct beaten into him over the last eight years. All he wanted to do was fall to his knees and spill everything he knew to the mother.

Mother Reina prowled, circling the three of them, a hungry predator's air pouring off her. Seth clenched his jaw so hard his bone ached when her wolf, maw dripping with saliva, nudged Ari with its nose.

Normally, it would take some urging from Seth for Ari to stay calm amid so many dominant creatures, but she barely stirred.

Mother Reina circled, slowly making her way before each of them. Her sightless white eyes bore into them as if she were looking straight past their defenses and pulling out their secrets with a sharpened claw.

She stopped before his father. "One of my

city's brightest minds," she took another step, heels clicking against the stone until she stood before his mother, "One of my most trusted department heads," another sharp step, and she stopped before Seth, snarling, "and my most promising initiate. All of them working in tandem to free one of the largest threats to Thaumoria mere minutes before her scheduled execution."

Seth stared straight ahead, schooling his features into a hard mask as he looked straight over the mother's head.

"She's gone. Out of your reach," his mother snarled, voice so low he didn't even know she could make such a sound.

The mother reeled on her. "You put your daughter above all my children. My entire city and all my people are at risk because of you."

"You were going to kill her for being different," his mother spit as if she weren't talking to the most powerful Anima Mother in recent history.

"It would have been a kindness. A swift execution to spare all Thaumoria. Or would you prefer we return to a time when an entire family line was exterminated for having borne a Dark Magic child?" Mother Reina's threat was a low growl that rumbled through Seth's chest.

A fierce, protective tension grew between the two mothers until even the council and a small host of guards squirmed with angst.

"You will not intimidate me into betraying my child," Mira breathed.

"And I will not be barred from protecting mine." Mother Reina held out a hand to no one in particular and flicked her fingers before turning away and approaching her council.

The few guards present closed in on Seth and his family, and finally, he moved. He stepped before his parents, holding out his arms as if he could shield them from what was to come.

"Daughter, might I suggest you rethink this?" the grandmother spoke up. Despite her words, there was no sympathy in the suggestions. Instead, the corner of her lip twisted at whatever idea she was waiting to unleash.

Mother Reina held out a palm, and the guards paused mere feet from Seth and his parents. His heart pounded in his chest, adrenaline flowing freely through his veins as he prepared to fight.

The grandmother approached slowly, her unnervingly giant scorpion perched on her shoulder. With a wicked gleam, she surveyed the small family.

"I understand the urge to eliminate traitors and those who threaten the safety of those in your care, but perhaps that isn't the correct approach. You wish to find this Mind Bender, no?"

Mother Reina's jaw clenched. "Yes, mother."

"If you execute her family or hold them in cells, she is guaranteed to hide forever. But if you punish them and send them back into the city, she will likely reach out. She will willingly expose herself, and much quicker than if you force her to hide."

Reina scowled, dipping her chin in the direction of the grandmother. "And how do I explain this to our people? That a Mind Bender walks among them? I am not Lord Kevah. I am not willing to let the Dark Magics haunt my streets and let my people live in fear."

"Of course not. We tell them we've executed the girl. No one outside this room needs to know the truth. You will have the girl in no time, and our people will be none the wiser." When Mother Reina didn't respond right away, turning the suggestion over in her mind, the grandmother added, "Sometimes we must lie to those we love to keep them safe."

With a heavy sigh that rippled through her dozen familiars, Mother Reina dropped her hand. She approached the family of three again, her tawny mountain lion by her side, her tail whipping back and forth with agitation.

"Your lives will be spared… for now." Seth nearly sagged with relief at the mother's declaration. "But do not think for a moment that there will not be repercussions. Both of you," she nodded toward his parents, her mountain lion's eyes narrowing as they bounced between the two still shielded behind his shoulders, "will be *heavily* demoted. I cannot have traitors in such influential positions in my city. And you, Seth," the mountain lion's eyes landed on him in tandem with the mother's, "I hope you enjoyed your time below ground, among the cells, because that is to be your permanent position for the rest of your time in my guard."

All the blood drained from Seth's face, and his lungs constricted until they barely took in air. Already, he felt the stone walls caving in on him.

Below ground… he was to spend the rest of his career, already pledged to the mother's service, down in the dimly lit dungeons. Every nerve in his body crawled, rejecting his new reality. He wasn't built for the dark, for the confinement. Seth thrived on freedom, on the ability to run through open fields and test his muscles on the obstacle course. Climbing and sprinting were his therapy, and now… now he would be as imprisoned as those he'd be guarding.

Mother Reina flicked her fingers at them. "Get them out of my sight."

The host of guards closed in again. Seth scooped up Ari from where she was still curled up on the stones as he and his parents were ushered toward the exit. Ari groaned but barely shifted in his arms, cradled close to his chest. He focused on her heartbeat, counting it as it beat in time with his own. His despair and her exhaustion flowed through their bond until every muscle in his body sagged.

With a small kiss between her ears, he headed straight for the estate's healer, flanked by his parents.

CHAPTER 7

Serena

One year later...

"Get back here!" someone boomed from between booths. The words echoed, the low ceilings of the dark market hidden beneath the City of Elementals' business district perfect for amplifying sounds.

Standing in the doorway of her makeshift kiosk, crammed between a Witch selling substances that could give an elephant enough energy to run a marathon and an Earth Wielder selling stolen gems, Serena searched for whoever was shouting. A moment later, a young girl broke through the slumped bodies of shoppers trying to go unnoticed, rat-eaten clothing hanging off her. She beelined for Serena, darting in her dark booth without a second thought.

Serena tipped her head to the side, her gaze following the girl, absently wondering what she'd stolen that time. A man barreled through patrons, face red with an anger that shoved itself down Serena's throat and forced her blood to buzz. Biting her lip, she tried to push the feeling away, but he emitted more emotion than most.

He stomped toward where she leaned against the crooked frame, arms crossed.

"Is she in there? I saw her run in there!" He pointed into the dimness of Serena's booth toward the young girl, doing her best to press herself into a shadowed corner.

Serena sighed through her nose before turning back to the red-faced man. Using a practiced, smooth voice, she looked the man up and down, forcing a sparkle into her green eyes. "Is there a problem?"

"That little thief stole my entire coin purse!" He made to push past Serena but paused when she placed a stern but gentle hand on his chest.

The initial shock of his anger slammed into her, but she refused to let it get below her skin before pushing it back. Through gritting teeth, she pushed her own indifference back at him, willing it to calm him.

"I'm sure," she cooed, "we can figure this out. Calmly."

With a heavy sigh, his rigid posture slackened. His anger wasn't gone, but it became controllable. Pliable.

Serena looked over her shoulder at the young girl whose frizzy brown hair poked out from beneath a hat pulled low on her head. The girl stared wide-eyed back and subtly shook her head, claiming her innocence, but Serena could practically see the girl's guilt buzzing around her like a gnat. She arched a scolding eyebrow, the same expression her mother used to give her, and the girl slumped. Serena held out a hand,

and the girl reluctantly handed over an embroidered leather bag jangling with coins.

She turned back to the man, holding out his coin purse. Her hand pressed to his chest moved to his arm, stoking it soothingly. "See? No harm, no foul."

His brows furrowed as he studied the bag, like he was hearing her words, knew they should bother him, but couldn't figure out why they didn't.

"Ok… but—but she should be punished?" he said it more like a question than a statement.

"Oh, yes. Of course. But first…" Delving deep within, Serena pulled forth the feeling of curiosity and longing and pushed it out toward him. "How about a reading?"

Her hold on the emotions were shaky at best, and they weren't as convincing as the indifference she'd previously been calling on.

The more she played with her magic, the more she understood how it worked, but she still didn't have a firm grasp on using or controlling it. Drudging up indifference enough to convince him of it as well was easy; she honestly did not care about his missing coin purse. But forcing herself to feel something she didn't was difficult on its own, let alone trying to thrust it upon another.

For the first time, he looked her up and down. Unimpressed by what he found, he practically snarled. "Reading? What does an Anima know about telling a person's future?"

Serena forced a coy smile and pushed the desire even harder, hoping just a thread would wind its way into his heart. "Let's call it animal intuition."

He glanced over her shoulder, once again narrowing in on the girl.

Grabbing his hand, Serena did her best to draw his attention back to her. "Completely free. My treat."

He hesitated, his skepticism wrapping its fingers around her muscles, pulling them taut against her bones.

"Fine," he grumbled.

"Wonderful," she beamed before turning around and internally sighed with relief. *Run,* she mouthed to the girl still cowering in the corner.

The girl didn't need any more prompting. She took off, darting out of the booth and delving into the dark market until she melted between people.

THE "READING" had taken a lifetime and was borderline painful. Serena's fortune-telling involved less seeing into the future and more reading and manipulating emotions through "palm reading" until she figured out what her customer wanted to hear. The man was a glutton for power and influence, and even the mere suggestion of hard times had made him murderous. Usually, she could play off a person's love for their family, children, or spouse by telling them about upcoming good news or strife in a relationship. But he hadn't been interested in any of those. Impatience and frustration were all she found when she mentioned his family. All he wanted to hear about was the success of his business dealings and the downfall of his competitors.

The moment he stepped out of her cramped booth, breathing became easier. He turned right, heading back the way he'd come, and she fell back into her chair with a huff of relief.

"Is he gone?" a small voice squeaked, peeking around the frame of her booth.

Serena sighed. "Yes, he's gone."

The young girl from earlier stepped into the booth, fidgeting with the torn hem of her shirt. "I'm sorry. I didn't think he'd notice."

Serena arched an eyebrow so high it nearly passed her hairline. "You didn't think he'd notice you stealing *all* his money?"

The girl shrugged, toeing the dirt floor. "I thought I was getting better."

"I think you need to find a new profession."

The girl nodded, then pulled an envelope from her pocket and held it out. Suspicious, Serena stared at the envelope, noticing how the girl's hands were better groomed than the rest of her would imply. She'd always seemed healthier than the other children, pale cheeks full and blushed with color. As if she wore her dirty appearance like a costume, rather than everyday attire.

"What's that?"

"It's for you."

Narrowing her eyes, she watched the girl carefully, trying to decipher her emotions from those of the others packed into the underground labyrinth.

"Who's it from? Did you write it?" It was mostly rhetorical since most of the children running around down there couldn't read or write.

"He just said to give it to you." The girl watched her with large round eyes that reminded Serena of a puppy begging for forgiveness.

Leaning closer, Serena noticed her name scrawled across the front in perfect handwriting. She snatched the envelope from the girl's hands and studied her name until it shook so badly it was nothing but a blur.

"Who wrote this? How does he know my

name?" she whispered, unwilling to let anyone know that someone knew who she actually was.

But the girl only dashed out of the booth, once again melding into the crowd before Serena could stop her.

Without waiting, Serena hung a blanket over the entrance of her booth, closing the shop for the day. It wasn't often she lit the gas lantern she'd long ago bartered for, fearful of wasting any precious resources, but she opened the valve completely. Shadows danced in its glow and she sat on her sagging cot pushed against the back of her booth. It wasn't much, but it kept her off the ground at night.

She took a deep breath and opened the envelope to find a small piece of paper no bigger than her palm, with a location and time written on it. That was it. Flipping the paper over and over, she searched every inch for a hidden message and found none.

Just a location not too far from the southern entrance to the dark market and a time that was quickly approaching. Time was stagnant below ground, easy to lose track of, as if it wasn't happening at all. But the Kinetic across the way sold stolen devices Serena regularly admired. Including the watches on display that told her she would need to leave soon to make the meeting.

Pausing, Serena shook her head. She was acting like she was actually going to *go* to the meeting with a strange man.

But he knew her name…

Names were sacred in the dark market, held close to the heart for fear of someone using it as currency against you. If anyone knew who she really was, they could take her name to the nearest city guard and sell her life for a few coins.

Frantic, she gathered what little belongings she had and stuffed them into the canvas and cotton bag she'd brought to the City of Elementals. If she was about to be exposed, she would be prepared to run. The dark market had been her home for nearly a year since she'd arrived in the City of Elementals. It was where she'd practiced her magic, trying through hours of excruciating trial and error to control it. It wasn't cozy or welcoming, but it had been hers, and it had been safe.

It was after sundown when she stepped foot onto the streets of the City of Elementals, mere feet above the market she left behind. Silently, she thanked the mysterious stranger for choosing a time after dark. The dark market wasn't ever completely devoid of light; since it ran all day and night, they always kept the lamps low. Stepping out into broad daylight after spending days underground blinded her every time.

After a few turns, Serena entered an alley between two brick buildings. Stopping just beyond the entrance, she sent her magic deep into the shadows, searching for ill intentions. She couldn't see the man hidden in the darkness beyond the light of the streetlamps, but she could feel him.

Patience and an innocent type of genuine curiosity met her magic, drawing her further into the alley. "Hello, Serena."

Hearing her name for the first time in a year nearly made her jump out of her skin.

"Who are you?" She croaked, refusing to let fear silence her, though she couldn't keep her words from quivering.

Slowly, her eyes adjusted, and a man in a perfectly pressed gray suit appeared. He stood far outside arm's reach, and she couldn't tell if it was for her comfort or his own.

"My name is Malachi. I have an offer for you." When he spoke, his words were slow, even, and sure. Almost devoid of any intonation at all. But Serena knew there was nothing dark lurking beneath the monotonous tone.

"How do you know my name?" She whispered, unwilling to let the issue go. Shifting from foot to foot, she was prepared to run at a moment's notice.

"Your name spread quite quickly after your… accusation in the City of Anima. It is not often someone with Dark Magic lives as long as you." If she weren't already sure by his stoic face, gray-green eyes, and near-colorless features, the clinical way he talked as if she were something to study made it clear he was a Kinetic.

"I don't have Dark Magic," she rushed, memories of being sentenced to execution clawing their way to the front of her mind.

Goosebumps rose along her skin when he laughed. It wasn't a condescending laugh, but almost a self-deprecating one. "No, no, you do not. Believe me, I have become quite adept at identifying it."

"Then why…" her words trailed off, unsure which question to ask.

"I am looking for someone to run a new branch of my business."

She shook her head. "Why me? I don't know anything about running a business." Which was mostly true. Of course, she ran her booth in the dark market, but that wasn't a *real* business. There were no books to keep or employees to watch over—just her, the client, and the person who ran the whole thing. A shiver ran down her spine at the thought of them.

"From what I understand, you are exactly the person I am looking for. I need someone with a taste for gathering and dealing in secrets and will be fiercely protective of those working for them."

Serena fidgeted with the strap of her bag, too preoccupied with her roiling emotions to pick apart his. Anxiety knotted itself within her chest, wrapping around her heart. "What kind of business is this?"

"I am looking for someone to help me turn informants into courtesans." The words were tight, and the uncomfortable stench of unease rolled off his tongue.

"Courtesans…" she tasted the word, her mind spinning. "You want me to sell people for sex?" Horror overtook her, and she had to reel herself back in before it poured out of her.

"No. At least, not how you think." He rushed through the explanation, and she could feel how they comforted him. He clearly had his own distaste for such a practice. "This is not a brothel; no one would ever be forced to do it. Those interested see sex as a means to an end. I, however, see how clients may… abuse this type of service. I will not allow that to happen."

"As a means to *what* end if sex isn't the point?"

"They are informants. They deal in secrets. I present you with the same question they presented to me: what better way to extract a person's darkest secrets than to seduce them and earn their most intimate trust?"

Serena pondered the question. "So why me? Why not choose one of them? An internal promotion, if you will. Or do it yourself."

"There are various reasons I do not wish to do it myself, the most important of which is undivided attention. I have too many responsibilities as it is, and there is no way for me to dedicate all my attention to this one branch. I will not stand for it to get any less. I need… a mother, if you will."

"But why *me*?"

The corner of his lips lifted in the smallest of smirks. "I have been keeping tabs on you for quite some time now, Serena. You may be familiar with a friend of mine?"

The young girl from the market peered

around the corner of an inset doorway, giving Serena a small wave.

"She… she works for you." No wonder the girl appeared so well-fed.

"Yes. I have been told you are very protective of those in need and that you have a gift for working with people. For seeing their inner desires and intentions and persuading them however you wish."

Serena sighed, staring down at her hands. "Yeah… my magic. It works… differently."

"I would be very interested in learning exactly what you mean by that, should you allow me."

Serena bit her lip, her glance bouncing between Malachi and the girl who half hid behind him. The girl's head bobbed with vigor, eyes gleaming as she urged Serena to say yes.

Hearts are our guides: listen, and you'll never be lost.

Her father's words whispered through her mind. She clung to the ghost of his voice and did her best to listen. Her heart thudded a steady rhythm in her chest. As if it was already at home with the new prospect.

"I'll have some conditions," she blurted. If she was going to do it, she would do it her way.

Malachi smiled, a soft, almost non-existent smile that was common in Kinetics. His satisfaction and understanding were so great she could taste them in the air, sweet and mild, like she'd said exactly what he'd wanted to hear. "I would be disappointed if you did not."

Acknowledgments

This novella was indeed one of the most difficult for me to write. As someone who struggles with anxiety, Serena's struggles often hit a little too close to home. I spent a lot of time thinking about the internal experience of my own mental health journey, and because of this, I often put it off. Now that it's here, though, I realize just how cathartic Serena's journey was to write.

As always, I want to start by thanking my husband, who has supported me unconditionally through my publishing journey. None of this would be a reality without you.

Next, to my editor. Sydney always goes above and beyond to help bring my stories to life.

To my cover designers, who couldn't have created a more beautiful depiction of Serena.

To my family for being endlessly supportive. The strong women of my family were the inspiration for this world, and I have no doubt they would fight tooth and nail for their kids.

Finally, I want to express my gratitude to you, the reader. This publishing journey was unlike any other, and it was your unwavering support that kept me going. The incredible backing from the book community has been a source of inspiration, and I look forward to continuing to provide stories that hopefully captivate and transport you.

Forever grateful,

A.M. Eno

About the Author

Originally from Howell, Michigan, A.M. Eno travels full-time with her husband and cat. In 2017, she earned her Bachelor of Science from Black Hills State University, majoring in Psychology and a minor in Sociology. As a life-long avid reader, she hopes to create worlds and characters that invite readers to fall in love and feel at home. She strives to write high fantasy series that are a safe space for people of all backgrounds.

www.authorameno.com